KU-600-092

Other books by Marion Gamble:

Moon Cat (2013)

Jack Wants a Pet (2014)

The Westwood Troll (2015)

For Jack, William and Alistair with love

Jack was in bed when he heard a strange noise.
Tap, tap tapping, tap, tap tapping.
He called for his mummy.
"Mummy, Mummy, can you come quickly."

"Yes Jack, what is it?"

"I can hear a strange noise," said Jack.

"A strange noise, what kind of strange noise?"

"I can hear a tap, tap tapping noise,"

"Well, maybe it's the wind in the trees."

"I think it's a Boody Monster," said Jack.

"A Boody Monster, what's a Boody Monster?"

"It's a hairy, scary purple monster that makes tap, tap tapping noises in the night.
He could be hiding in the garden and give us all a fright."

"If there's a monster in our garden, perhaps he's looking for a home.
If he's from around this neighbourhood, who knows where he
might roam.
He couldn't live at our house, we just don't have the room.
A hairy scary purple monster, that might not be much fun."

Jack's mummy looked out of the window, the moon was shining bright.
"I can't see any Boody Monster, there's no need for a fright."

Jack's mummy locked the window and drew the curtains tight.
"It's time to go to sleep Jack," and she kissed Jack goodnight!

The next day Jack, his mummy and his two brothers William and Alistair went to play in the park and they took a picnic for tea.

They went to Winda Woppa, a playground by the sea.
With swings and slides and roundabouts nestling in the trees.

They spread their picnic on the ground and there they had their tea.

Jack was playing on the swings when he heard a strange noise.

"Coo-ee, coo-ee, coo-ee."

He called for his mummy.

"Mummy, Mummy can you come quickly?"

"Yes Jack, what is it?"

"I can hear a strange noise," said Jack.

"A strange noise, what kind of strange noise?"

"I can hear a coo-ee, coo-ee noise."

Jack's mummy listened and she too could hear a strange noise.

A coo-ee, coo-ee noise was drifting on the breeze.

"I can hear that coo-ee, coo-ee noise," she said, "well maybe it's a bird in the trees."

"I think it's a Boody Monster," said Jack.

"A Boody Monster, what's a Boody Monster?"

"It's a hairy, scary purple monster that makes coo-ee noises in the park."

Jack's mummy looked all around in corners that were dark.
"I can't see any Boody Monster, he must be hiding for a lark."

Then Jack climbed up the slippery dip and looked out across the sea.
He spied the Boody Monster hiding high up in a tree.
"I can see the Boody Monster, quick Mummy, come and see."

Jack's mummy saw the Boody Monster high above the ground.
There is a Boody Monster and now he has been found.

He lives at Winda Woppa, he's found a home at last.
And whenever we go along that way, we'll wave as we go past.

If you hear a Boody Monster making coo-ee noises in the park.
Or if he comes to your house tap, tapping after dark.

I'm sure he is friendly, he doesn't scratch or bite.
If he comes calling to your house, it's just to say 'Goodnight'!